TEAM HERO

RISE OF THE SHADOW SNAKES

ADAM BLADE

ORCHARD

MEET TEAM HERO ...

JACK

POWER: Super-strength
LIKES: Ventura City FC
DISLIKES: Bullies

RUBY

POWER: Fire vision
LIKES: Comic books
DISLIKES: Small spaces

DANNY

POWER: Super-hearing and sonic blast
LIKES: Pizza
DISLIKES: Thunder

Special thanks to Michael Ford

ORCHARD BOOKS

First published in Great Britain in 2018 by The Watts Publishing Group

1 3 5 7 9 10 8 6 4 2

Text © 2018 Beast Quest Limited
Cover and inside illustrations by Dynamo
© Beast Quest Limited 2018

Team Hero is a registered trademark in the European Union
Series created by Beast Quest Limited, London

A CIP catalogue record for this book is available from the British Library.

ISBN 978 1 40834 365 4

Printed in Great Britain

Orchard Books
An imprint of Hachette Children's Group
Part of The Watts Publishing Group Limited
Carmelite House, 50 Victoria Embankment, London EC4Y 0DZ

An Hachette UK Company
www.hachette.co.uk
www.hachettechildrens.co.uk

...ND THEIR GREATEST ENEMY

GENERAL GORE

POWER: Brilliant warrior

LIKES: Carnage

DISLIKES: Unfaithful minions

CONTENTS

OLLY FLEW through the deserted corridors of Valour Station. With most of the other students on patrol in Solus, or recovering in the infirmary, the Team Hero base was as silent as a crypt.

And that suits me fine, he thought.

He reached the dormitory and drifted inside, landing beside his bed.

He peeled off his damaged skysuit, melted away in sections by Quilla the Falcon of Fury. Not that he'd needed the suit in the first place. Of all the powers possessed by Team Hero, his was the best — the ability to fly!

Turning to face the mirror on his wardrobe door, Olly admired the silver breastplate he wore over his torso. Swirls of red, like channels of cooling lava, decorated the surface. *The Flameguard.* A sacred artefact, kept in the Solus vaults for centuries.

It had protected him from General Gore's fiery attack, but what else could it do? He couldn't wait to find out. Jack and his annoying do-gooder friends had tried to warn him the Flameguard was dangerous, but it was obvious why. *They just want it for themselves.*

   "Well, I'd like to see them try to take it," said Olly, grinning at his own reflection.

   Jack had been a nuisance since the first day he arrived at Hero Academy. All the staff and students loved him. They practically bowed down and worshipped at his feet. Even Chancellor Rex, the headteacher. He seemed to think Jack was the so-called Chosen One, the hero prophesied to save them all from General Gore.

They've not seen anything yet! thought Olly, stroking the gleaming breastplate. Jack might have weird, strong hands, but Olly knew that the Flameguard would make him the most powerful Hero who'd ever lived.

"Why be a hero?" whispered a voice.

Olly frowned. At first he thought the voice must have come from Buzzard, his Oracle device. But as he reached for his ear, he realised it was switched off.

"You could rule the world," whispered the voice again.

The words seemed to come from somewhere in his chest. Right under the Flameguard.

Suddenly, Olly didn't want to wear the breastplate anymore. He reached for the clasps at his side, only to find them shut tight. Panicking, he tugged harder. The fastenings wouldn't loosen. If anything, they *tightened*.

Then something happened in the mirror. Olly gazed in horror as the red tendrils across the breastplate began to glow, spreading across his chest and neck like red veins. More snaked along his arms. Olly staggered, eyes wide. But as the tingling heat surged

through his limbs, a new feeling
spread with it. *Power* ... He found
himself smiling as the red branches
travelled up his face. His eyes went
bloodshot, then completely red, then

back to normal again.

"We can do anything now," said the voice, booming inside his head.

CHAPTER 1

HISSRAH

THIS PLACE should be a *paradise*, thought Jack, gazing around at the Herptamon city. Painted domes, ringed with coiling terraces, spread out among the leafy oasis. The air was filled with the scent of flowers and ripe fruit.

But a cold wind blew among the

trees, and foliage that should have been vivid green was cast in shade. Jack stared at the Starstone, floating over the Great Pyramid in the middle of Solus. Once it had blazed, throwing a golden glow over the four cities. Now it was almost entirely infected by the shadow of General Gore. Only a sliver of light remained, and Jack let it bathe his face.

It might be the last time I ever feel it.

For days he'd watched the shadow growing, despair creeping over his heart. If they didn't stop it soon, and the blackness took over completely, it wasn't just the four cities of Solus that would suffer. There'd be nothing to prevent Gore's shadow infecting the entire world.

Ruby's voice spoke through Hawk, the Oracle device in his ear.

"We don't have long, Jack. How's it going?"

Professor Yokata and most of the Team Hero squad based at Valour Station were out of action, injured in the previous battles against Gore's forces. Ruby and Danny were stationed inside the Pyramid with the few others who remained, guarding the Solus leaders as they worked desperately to fashion a new

Starstone — only its pure light could permanently defeat the shadows of Noxx.

"Almost done," said Jack.

He stood beneath the coiled stone cobra that the Herptamon called Hissrah. The Guardian Statue had stood in the centre of the city for a thousand years, worshipped by the snake-like citizens. So far, three of the four cities of Solus had fallen into darkness. Each time the eclipse reached their Guardian Statues, they came to life, turned from mythical protectors into deadly foes controlled by General Gore. It was only a matter of time before Hissrah did the same.

That was why they were going to blow her up.

Jack, along with a few other Team Hero students, watched as the warriors of the four cities finished laying explosive charges around the base of the giant cobra. The scorpion-like Tavnar, the cat-people of Leoriah and the winged Avaretti worked together with the scaly Herptamon. The four races had been at peace for centuries, hidden from the rest of the human world. And they were united against their common enemy, General Gore. However, Jack saw one of the

snake-faced warriors looking worried
as he whispered to a Tavnar soldier.

"Hissrah brings trust and friendship
to all of
Solus,"
he said,
checking a
fuse line.
"What
happens if
we destroy
her?"

"We must,"
said the
armoured
scorpion-woman, her arched tail

drooping. "The elders command it."

"They're just doing what Team Hero command," said the snake-soldier, fingering the whip that was looped into his belt. "But I don't know who put these humans in charge. They're not even from Solus."

"It's the only option," said Jack, interrupting so everyone could hear. "You've seen already what happens when Gore's poisonous shadow infects a statue."

With a few lingering doubtful looks, the work continued. Jack could hardly blame the citizens of Solus for their lack of faith in him. After all, he was just a boy — a stranger. Chancellor Rex thought he was the Chosen One — the hero meant to fight the darkness — but sometimes he wasn't so sure.

Jack saw the shadow creeping closer. "Stand back!" he ordered, then went behind one of the nearby buildings to the detonation controls. The soldiers scattered to a safe distance. With a last look at the snake's proud profile, rearing as if to watch over the entire city, Jack flicked the switch.

BOOM!

He turned and covered his face with his arm as he felt the blast wave hit. The ground shook beneath his feet.

Sand and dust rained down. When Jack looked back, where the statue had stood was now a heap of rubble. The Herptamon warriors bowed their heads, and Jack felt their loss.

His heart skipped a beat as the rubble shifted a little.

"Good work, Jack," came Danny's voice in his ear. "At least the city's safe now."

Jack looked back to the debris pile, but the movement had stopped. *Must just have been settling.*

"I hope we did the right thing," Jack replied. "Any luck finishing the new Starstone?"

A pause. "No," said Danny. "There's an ingredient the leaders can't find. A *Heart of Fire*, whatever that means."

"Keep looking," said Jack.

One of the Leoriah screamed. Jack turned to see that the cat-soldier had something coiled around his ankle. *A black snake!* Then the ground seemed to seethe. The chunks of broken statue that had fallen into shadow were all moving — melting — and each one grew into a snake. Some were normal sized, but others were several metres long, as thick as Jack's leg.

Our plan hasn't worked. Gore's shadow is even poisoning the debris!

Jack drew his sunsteel blade, Blaze, as the Herptamon unfurled their whips and the Avaretti stabbed with their spears. But hundreds of snakes were swarming across the ground.

"We've got a problem!" Jack said through Hawk. "Backup needed!"

He saw a snake around the neck of one Avaretti, and another coiling across the flailing stinger of a Tavnar. Cries of pain rose up from all around as the snakes' fangs sank into their victims, finding the gaps in their armour. Jack hacked at a shadow snake with his sword, cutting it in two. It dissolved into black dust. He danced between the attackers, chopping and swiping.

One of the snakes darted at his leg. He caught it with his super-strong hands and squeezed. The snake exploded into crumbling, ash-like powder. But more were coming,

from every direction. Jack stooped
and grabbed a boulder that must
have weighed half a tonne. His hands
shone gold with power as he tossed
the boulder on top of the snakes,
crushing five or six. It didn't stop
the others, but it bought him a few
seconds, and he scrambled up on
to the remains of the plinth where
Hissrah had stood.

From his vantage point, he scanned
the eyes of those who'd been bitten,
expecting them to turn black with
evil poison. He'd seen the shadow
infection turn innocent people into
mindless minions of Gore.

To his surprise, they did not. They looked about themselves in confusion, seemingly unharmed, as the snakes released them. One by one, the snakes darted for the plinth where Jack was standing, climbing up all four sides

like a wriggling wave of black.

"Help me!" Jack called to the Solus
soldiers standing around.

"Why should we?" replied a bird-
warrior, flapping his wings angrily.

"Get a Herptamon to help you," said

a scorpion-woman. "They're nothing but belly-crawlers."

A snake-warrior lashed at her. "Watch what you're saying, or I'll rip that stinger off!"

A cat-soldier of the Leoriah pounced and landed on one of the Avaretti, raking with his claws and snarling. "This is your fault, bird-brain! If you lot spent less time preening your feathers and more time practising with your weapons, we wouldn't be in this mess."

Jack kicked a snake off the edge of the plinth, then slashed at another, but he could see it was a hopeless

 battle. The tide kept coming.

"What's wrong with you all?" he cried. "We're meant to work together!"

"I'm not working with a whiskered coward!" said the scorpion-woman, darting her stinger at the Leoriah soldier. "It was the cat-folk who got the Starstone infected."

What's happening? They're turning against one another.

And then he remembered! Hissrah

was supposed to keep the Solus races at peace.

He spun round, as more snakes poured towards him. He felt something tighten around his ankle, and tripped up on to his back. A snake slithered up his leg as more pressed closer.

Jack defended himself as the creatures lunged for him, but even as he fought them off, he knew that he and his friends had more than snakes to worry about.

We destroyed the statue and now all of Solus will turn on each other!

One snake tightened around his

wrist, and Jack let go of Blaze.
Another circled his limbs like ice-cold
chains, pinning him to the ground.

They're toying with me . . .

As he fought to free himself,
another slithering shadow crept up
his chest. The snake coiled around his
neck, gently at first. It reared up, its
neck fanning just like Hissrah's, over
his head. The empty black eyes fixed
on Jack's face as the snake squeezed
its body.

Jack struggled to draw a breath
but couldn't. Black spots clouded his
vision.

The snake squeezed tighter still . . .

CHAPTER 2

EVIL RISES AGAIN

THE BLACK snake looming over Jack turned suddenly yellow, then orange, then red, like an ember heated in the fire. Then it burst into black smoke. Jack drew in a huge breath and twisted his head sideways. Ruby stood nearby, eyes glowing with power.

She used her fire beams!

"Thought you needed help," she said.

"Cover your ears!" said Danny, arriving through the trees beside her.

Jack clamped his hands around his head. He saw Danny open his mouth, and *felt* the blast of supersonic energy coming from his friend. As well as having hearing a thousand times better than a normal person, Danny could release intense sound waves. The snakes covering Jack's body trembled from head to tail, then exploded into clouds of dusty ash.

"Thanks!" said Jack. He stood up weakly. Thousands of snakes still crawled across the oasis, and the air was filled with battle cries as the Solus soldiers fought each other.

"Don't let the snakes bite you!" said Jack. "Their venom turns friend against friend."

Ruby swept her fire-gaze in an arc around her feet as the shadow snakes edged towards her. Danny wiped out others with his sonic cries. But Jack knew that both of them would run out of strength eventually. He grabbed Blaze and leapt down from the plinth, carving a path through the slithering mass of snakes to stand back to back with his friends.

Ruby smashed the rim of her

mirrored shield on to a snake, severing it in half. Danny roared again, but this time it only drove the snakes back a few feet. When they recovered they pressed forwards once more, like a black slick of oil, pushing them back.

We're fighting a losing battle.

Jack felt his back touch something solid and realised they'd been forced against the wall of one of the domed Herptamon dwellings. Steep and smooth, there was no way to climb it.

"This is it, guys!" he said. "We fight until our last breath."

His friends nodded grimly. If Jack was going to die, there was no one he'd rather have beside him. And if they could buy the Solus elders more time to complete the Starstone, the sacrifice was worth it.

"Hey!" cried a familiar voice. "You losers need a hand?"

Jack glanced up and saw Olly hovering overhead. Their fellow student didn't need a skysuit, because flying was his special power. He was, however, wearing the silver breastplate stolen from the Pyramid vault, the ancient artefact the Solus leaders called the Flameguard.

Olly spread his arms wide and the breastplate glowed, casting a wave of red light towards the ground. In an instant, hundreds of shadow snakes shrivelled and disintegrated under the glare. Jack had disliked Olly from the time they first met, but just then, he'd never been so happy to see anyone.

"Pretty amazing, right?" said Olly, landing beside them and tapping the Flameguard with a fist.

Jack glanced at his friends. "You need to give that back, Olly," he said.

Olly's face twisted into a scowl. "Oh, really? Says who?"

"You stole it!" said Ruby. "The Solus elders say the Flameguard isn't safe."

"They would say that," snapped Olly.

"But you'd have been snake food if it wasn't for me."

"Yes, and thank you," said Jack patiently. "But Olly, listen. That breastplate will corrupt your mind."

"You're just jealous," said Olly, puffing out his chest. "Turns out I'm the Chosen One, not you!"

Darkness swept overhead, and Jack turned with the others to the Starstone. The last chink of its light had gone completely — the giant sun was a black ball. At the same time, Jack saw the distant glimmer of the human city of Khalea, several miles away across the Flammara desert.

And that was completely wrong, because it meant the protective dome concealing Solus from the outside world had vanished.

"We're too late," Jack mumbled under his breath.

He peered at the artificial sun of Solus. Looking carefully, he realised it wasn't simply black. It had a purplish tinge, and currents of dark energy seemed to course through its depths.

Gore's plan is complete. Now his evil can spread across the entire world.

The remaining snakes writhed too, slithering towards one another, then coiling around each other's bodies in a seething heap of reptilian flesh. Jack realised he could no longer see where one shadow ended and the other began. It was almost as if they were dissolving into one another, mirroring the black swirls on the surface of the corrupted Starstone.

"What's happening?" muttered Olly. His bravado seemed to have vanished.

A lumpen form was taking shape in the centre of the snakes, and as its edges revealed themselves, Jack choked back a cry of terror. It was man — a giant — hunched over in a crouch. Dread crept over Jack's skin. He already knew who it was.

The figure stood proud amid the shadow snakes. They hissed as one, welcoming their master. Jack felt Ruby and Danny pressing closer to his side as the man drew a deep, satisfied breath. It was as if he were breathing fresh air for the first time.

The snakes parted, and the massive warrior's black armour clanked as he walked slowly and heavily towards them. Spikes bristled across his gauntlets and shoulder plates.

Under the open faceguard of his black helmet, two eyes glowed the colour of fresh blood.

General Gore had returned.

CHAPTER 3

THE POISON SPREADS

JACK MARCHED past Olly, brandishing his sunsteel blade.

"If it isn't the Chosen One," rasped General Gore, his voice like rocks grating over one another. "You and your pathetic 'heroes' have failed this time. The Starstone is mine, and soon the entire world will belong to me too."

"You won't get out of Solus," said Jack.

General Gore laughed. "You cannot stop me."

Let's see about that . . .

Jack rushed at General Gore, swinging Blaze. The sword cut deep into Gore's shoulder, but the General didn't even cry out. Instead, he simply moved away, pulling the blade free. "It'll take more than a little sunsteel to harm me now."

"Try this!" said Ruby. Her orange jet of flame crashed into General Gore's chest, but passed straight through to the other side, scorching the ground.

*He's both shadow and solid at the
same time!*

"He's invincible!" Ruby whispered.

"Move aside," cried Danny.

They backed off, covering their ears,
and Danny drew back his shoulders
and bellowed. Jack saw the air ripple
with the sonic blast, and a split
second later Gore staggered, almost
lifted off his feet. But he drove his
heels into the ground and came to a
stop. His eyes blazed even brighter.
"Is that all you weaklings have? My
turn!"

General Gore raised his arms, and
his shadow-limbs stretched, forming

black blades each a metre long. He swung one, and Danny ducked beneath the scything weapon. Jack parried the other blade with his sword, but the force knocked him to his knees. Gore pressed on against Ruby, who lifted her shield to deflect the blows, but was sent sprawling too.

Jack picked himself up, fired by anger. He hacked at General Gore's ankle, but the blade passed harmlessly through the shadow. Gore lifted a foot and kicked, catching Jack in the chest. He flew through the air and crashed into a wall. The dark world seemed to spin.

How can I defeat him?

One of General Gore's sword-arms morphed into a war-hammer, and he stamped towards Jack's prone body.

As he was about to bring down the
massive weapon, a blast of red energy
smashed into his arm and spun him
round.

"Back off, Gore!" said Olly.
He floated above them all, the
Flameguard aglow.

Gore's eyes blazed. "You have
brought the breastplate to me!"

"Afraid not," said Olly. "I'm here to
show you what a real hero can do."

Another beam of light shot from the
Flameguard, but this time General
Gore held up his hand. It became
a round black shield, and the blast
simply fizzed out. Jack saw Olly's

eyes widen in shock as the shadow-shield transformed into a whip. Olly squealed as it snaked around him, trying to prise the Flameguard from his body. "Give it to me!" cried Gore.

He's distracted . . .

Jack ran at the General, slicing at the whip. "Get off him!"

The sunsteel blade severed it. Olly must have been pulling away hard, because he suddenly shot backwards, careering into a building fifty metres away and crashing out of sight.

Olly?

General Gore turned on Jack. "Enough games," he said. "Behold my power and see what awaits the human world."

Gore pointed towards the purple orb that had once been the Starstone. At once, tendrils began to expand from its surface like licking tongues. They split and multiplied, until there were hundreds, some reaching across the sky and others twisting down into the four cities of Solus. Jack saw people fleeing from the Pyramid. Like darting snakes, the black tendrils latched on to them, freezing the innocent in their tracks.

Ruby gasped. "What's the Starstone doing to them?"

"The Starstone is no more!" laughed Gore. "It is my Shadow Orb now. Where once it brought life, now it carries the curse of Noxx."

The purple-black tentacles whipped through the air, snagging on Team Hero students and Solus citizens alike. As they were touched, they spasmed for a moment, then fell. *Are they dead?* Jack wondered with a bolt of horror.

Ruby blasted a tentacle with her eyes, and it backed off like it had been burned. But more were coming. Another made a grab for Danny, and without thinking, Jack threw himself in its path. As it touched him, he felt a blast of cold through his veins, then nothing.

I'm still immune to the shadow. We still have a chance.

"Guys, regroup to me!" Jack called out.

Danny and Ruby came to his side, but General Gore simply laughed. "This is it, then. The final stand of Team Hero. Would you like to see what you will become?"

He stepped aside, to reveal hundreds of figures marching towards them. Avaretti, Tavnar, Herptamon and Leoriah. And among them, even a few Team Hero students.

But they walked oddly, hunched over and staggering. As they came closer, Jack swallowed in terror. The eyes of Gore's soldiers were black pits, their exposed skin mottled black as if bruised. The wings of the Avaretti were plucked half bare, leaving only sparse black feathers, and the lips of the Leoriah warriors were drawn back over discoloured fangs. Tavnar stingers dripped black poison and the Herptamon's scales looked shrivelled and dying.

An army of darkness, thought Jack. *Without mercy . . .*

He looked on helplessly, and felt

the hope draining from his friends
as well. There was no way they could
fight so many.

The sky overhead was gloomy,
with lightning flashing through the
purplish clouds. The black poison of
Noxx whipped and whirled, spreading
far beyond the city now. Soon it would
reach Khalea, corrupting the innocent
civilians. And from there, nothing
could stop it.

*General Gore's right. Our final
battle is about to begin.*

CHAPTER 4

WORLD OF DARKNESS

"THERE'S NOWHERE to hide," said
Gore. "Give yourself to my shadow . . .
Become my slaves."

"We'd rather die," said Ruby.

General Gore's eyes burned brighter.
"So be it." He stepped aside, making
way for the ranks of infected, who
began to charge.

Jack's eyes fell on the Solus Pyramid in the distance. If they could only reach the huge structure, it might offer some sanctuary — and the chance to come up with a plan to defeat Gore.

"We need to make a run for the Pyramid," he said to his friends.

"How?" asked Danny, waving a hand at the hundreds of soldiers marching towards them.

"We need to puncture a hole in their forces," said Jack. "And once we're through, we don't look back."

"Got it," said Ruby. "Let's start with a smoke screen."

She unleashed a sideways blast of fire. The beam scorched the earth a few metres in front of them, sending up a cloud of black smoke.

"Now run!" she said.

With his friends at his side, Jack charged towards the oncoming forces. Danny let rip with a sonic boom, and through the smoke, Jack saw bodies hurled into the air. He just hoped no one was badly hurt. *It's not their fault, what they're doing. They're not in control of themselves . . .*

Jack and his friends plunged into the drifting smoke. A Tavnar turned on him, mouth stretching horribly

wide, and stabbed with her pincer.
Poison dripped from the tip. Jack
caught it between his golden hands,
and with a lurch, he swung the
creature into a crowd of Avaretti. He
sprinted after Ruby through a gap
Danny had opened in a row of Leoriah.

"After them!" roared General Gore. "They're getting away."

Gore's infected ranks began to recover, but Jack was already sprinting between the Herptamon dwellings. Ruby moved in darting runs, pausing to lay down smokescreens behind them. Jack looked for a way through to the Pyramid. Above it, the dark purple shadow orb throbbed like a demented eye, its tentacles reaching into the cities below, snaring more innocent people of Solus.

Jack skidded to a halt as he saw a black tongue of shadow sneaking around a building ahead. He tugged his friends down an alley, but another tendril awaited them.

"We're being surrounded," said Ruby. "Jack, you'll have to go on alone. You're the only one who's immune to shadow."

"No way," said Jack. "I'm not leaving you."

"Wait!" said Danny, twitching his bat-like ears. "I can hear something." He began to tiptoe between buildings, Jack and Ruby following.

Then Jack heard it too — a groan. It was coming from beneath a collapsed wall. A pair of dust-covered legs were sticking out, wearing the silver Team Hero uniform.

Power flowed into Jack's hands, and he gripped the base of the fallen wall. He was about to hoist it off the student, when a fist smashed the bricks from below, and Olly, still wearing the Flameguard, scrambled out.

"Oh, it's you guys," he said.

"How did you do that?" asked Ruby, looking at the huge weight Olly had escaped from beneath.

"The Flameguard, of course," said Olly proudly. "I'm even stronger than Jack now."

They heard the patter of rushing footsteps, and a Tavnar skidded around the corner, followed by a Leoriah, both of them holding spears.

"Let me handle this," said Olly. He faced their enemies and his breastplate shone red. Jack shoved him just in time, and the Flameguard's death-ray slammed into a nearby wall, incinerating it.

"Hey!" said Olly.

"We can't just kill them!" said Jack. "They're innocent people under Gore's control!"

"Do you have a better idea?" said Olly. He jumped into the air and hovered above them. "Because I don't plan on waiting around to get turned into one of Gore's zombies."

"Wait!" said Danny. "Maybe you can give us all a lift?"

Olly's face split into a smug grin as Herptamon soldiers appeared on a roof opposite. Jack and his companions were being surrounded.

"Come on then," said Olly, flying up to hover higher above them. "Hold on."

Jack grabbed hold of Olly's ankles, and felt his weight leave the ground easily. Danny and Ruby seized Jack's lower legs, before Olly lifted them up and away from the Herptamon, dodging the black shadows licking from the infected Starstone.

As they flew over Solus, Jack looked down in despair at the four cities shrouded in darkness. General Gore was nowhere to be seen, but his army swarmed everywhere. It wouldn't be

long until every single citizen of Solus had fallen under Gore's thrall.

"We've let them all down," he whispered. "We've failed, and the human world might be next."

Olly carried them towards the top of the Great Pyramid, right beneath the corrupted Starstone.

"There are the elders!" cried Ruby.

Jack saw Queen Felina, the half-cat leader of the Leoriah, and the other leaders of the Solus peoples gathered by a gateway on one of the upper steps. They were surrounded by a detachment of royal guards. Queen Felina's sister Ms Steel, a teacher from Hero Academy, stood with them. She was in her cat form too.

Olly flew low over the Pyramid. "This is your stop," he said. Danny and Ruby dropped down beside the elders, and Jack released his grip too.

The Tavnar leader pointed at Olly, still hovering out of reach. "He has the Flameguard! Thief!"

"If it wasn't for me, these three would be dead," said Olly. "Be grateful I'm on your side."

"You must take it off," said the Herptamon elder, his scaled face creased with concern. "The Flameguard will consume you."

"I know what I'm doing, thanks," said Olly. "You should have seen Gore's face when he laid eyes on it!"

"You do not understand," said the Avaretti elder firmly. "The Flameguard is no ordinary weapon. It has a mind and will of its own."

"We don't have time for this now," said Queen Felina. She cast aside her robes and took out a grey rock, only as big as an apple. "We need to find the final ingredient for the new Starstone."

Oh, thought Jack, trying not to frown. *Is that it?*

"Doesn't look like much!" said Olly.

"We still need the *Heart of Fire*," said

Felina, "whatever that is. The scrolls with the instructions for its creation were not clear."

Danny's eyes widened, and he pointed to Olly. "Perhaps it's the Flameguard!"

Olly flew up even further. "No chance. This is mine."

"Don't be a fool!" said Ms Steel. "Listen to yourself, Olly — the power is already corrupting you."

As she spoke, Jack's eyes were drawn to the cities below.

"We've got a problem," he said.

The forces of General Gore were on the move, but not towards the

Pyramid. They teemed through the
streets and out into the desert —
in the direction of the human city
of Khalea. The shadow from the
Starstone seemed to spread with
them, a tide of night reaching across
the desert towards the city.

"How can we stop so many?" said
Queen Felina.

"I don't know, but we have to try,"
said Jack.

"We might be able to warn the
people of Khalea what's heading their
way," said Ruby.

Jack spoke to his Oracle. "Hawk, get
a message to Valour Station at once."

"Sorry, Jack. There's some electromagnetic interference."

"Channels are down," Jack told the others. He looked up at the tongues of shadow spreading from the corrupted Starstone. "It must be Gore's Shadow Orb."

"There are spare skysuits inside the Pyramid," said Danny.

"We'll be too late," said Jack. "Someone needs to warn Khalea."

"Leave that to me," said Ms Steel. She donned her magical ring and returned to human form, then in the blink of an eye, she vanished.

She's teleported to the city, thought

Jack, full of hope. *If anyone can organise an evacuation, it's her.*

Jack turned towards the Pyramid entrance, and heard the flap of wings at his back. Suddenly hundreds of Avaretti filled the sky. But they were not the elegant bird-like beings he'd become accustomed to. Their wings didn't even have feathers anymore, but were black and leathery, like bat wings. Their beaked faces were cruel, and their talons glinted.

"No! Stop!" cried their ruler, taking flight.

None of his shadow-corrupted people listened, but three dived right

at him, slamming into his body and carrying him off into the distance. Jack could hardly bear to watch.

"Looks like Gore's sent his minions to finish us off," said Queen Felina.

CHAPTER 5

SHOWDOWN WITH GENERAL GORE

DANNY ROARED a sonic blast, scattering several of the corrupted Avaretti, while Olly sent another spiralling down the side of the Pyramid with a fierce punch.

"We must retreat deeper inside the pyramid," said the Tavnar ruler, lifting her stinger menacingly.

"The doors won't hold forever," said the Herptamon elder.

"They don't need to," said Queen Felina grimly. "We just need long enough to finish the Starstone while my sister and Team Hero defeat General Gore."

"*If* they can defeat him," said the snake elder.

"We will," said Jack, though he had no idea if that was true.

Queen Felina tucked the grey Starstone under her robes again. "Good luck," she said. "Solus's fate rests with you now."

Jack donned his skysuit quickly, as Olly sent out warning shots to keep the corrupted Avaretti at bay. Once he was zipped in, he, Danny and Ruby took off.

"Olly, you should come to Khalea too," he said. "That Shadow Orb is making Gore's army stronger with every step. We need all the help we can get!"

Olly shook his head as he wrestled with an Avaretti in mid-air. "They need me here too," he said. "I'll protect the Solus leaders while they finish the Starstone."

Strange . . . since when did Olly care about anyone but himself?

Jack was about to protest, but he

could see the shadow army creeping towards the outskirts of Khalea already. And Olly did seem to be doing a good job. He kicked the Avaretti in the chest and it shot backwards through the sky.

Jack turned and levelled his foot blasters, letting the skysuit's jets rocket him through the air. They flew in formation as the wreckage of the cities below gave way to the desert sands that lay between Solus and Khalea. The lights of the human city twinkled in the distance. Though it was only the middle of the afternoon, the sky was dark with shadow. From a distance, the city looked peaceful, but as they reached the outskirts, Jack saw the first signs of devastation. Scorched fields full of dead crops, then a dark highway cluttered with crashed and stalled vehicles. The trail of chaos and destruction was easy to follow, and soon they crossed over a park filled with shrivelled and rotting trees. Gore's foul shadow ruined everything it touched.

A few of Gore's army were still

marching through the parkland, and looked up, hissing and shouting, as Jack flew above. Skyscrapers loomed ahead; the glass of hundreds of windows had been shattered. A cold, gusting wind blew shadow through the buildings, scattering blackened papers like ash flakes. People poured from the ground floors to join Gore's army, moving with blank-eyed robotic steps.

The whole world will end up like this if we don't stop him.

Ahead, the central river of Khalea split the city in two. People and cars were racing across its bridge, trying to get to its far bank. Jack saw the lights of emergency vehicles gathering there. *Ms Steel must have spread the word quickly.* The police would try to make a stand, but it would be hopeless.

"Perhaps we can contain the horde if we take down the crossing," he called to the others.

"Destroy the bridge?" said Danny. "But . . . "

"There's no other way," said Ruby. "We'll have to close the tunnel too. My oracle says there's an underpass. Maybe we can flood it." She pointed, and Jack saw the tunnel opening.

"We can't do that!" said Danny. "There'll be people down there."

Jack saw a number of abandoned lorries on the road. "I've got another idea. You guys deal with the bridge."

Ruby and Danny veered off towards the crossing, while Jack travelled down to the underpass. Back over his shoulder he saw Ruby's eye-beams streaming onto the bridge's cables, while Danny used his sound waves to blast the army trying to cross.

Jack landed beside a truck, summoning all his strength into his scaly hands. With a roar, he heaved the truck into position, blocking the tunnel entrance.

That should hold the army off for

a while. At least until the innocent
civilians on the other side can
evacuate.

"Oh, look who it is!" said a voice. Jack
turned to see two figures marching
towards him. One was tall and thin, his
sharp-featured face half-hidden under

a hood. It was Gore's sorcerer, Smarm. The other, Bulk, was short, fat and bald, with flab squeezing out through the gaps in his leather armour. He held a double-headed axe.

Jack sighed. He didn't have time to deal with them right now. "It's over," he said. "Gore's army stops here."

Bulk tittered, and spittle drooled over his thick lips. "It's only just begun," he said. With a yell, he charged at Jack, swinging the heavy axe. Jack leapt into the air as Bulk careered head-first into the truck, flopping to the ground.

Smarm ignited a ball of purple

energy in his palm and sent it flying towards Jack. He dodged as the projectile smashed into a streetlight, making it buckle in the centre. As the top section began to fall, Jack gripped it and tore it free, wielding it like a baseball bat. But the moment before it hit Smarm, the sorcerer disappeared. Bulk too had vanished.

I guess I'll be seeing those two again, Jack thought, as he dropped the pole and flew up to join Ruby and Danny. They were hovering above the bridge, watching the ranks of Gore's army stalled on the banks below.

Gore himself appeared behind them.

"Swim, you idiots!" he bellowed.

One by one, the soldiers jumped into the water, beginning to swim across.

"They'll do anything he says," said Danny, gaping.

With a sinking heart, Jack realised that they had about five minutes before the soldiers reached the far side and the invasion continued.

But Gore stands alone, he thought. *Unprotected . . .*

"Maybe if we deal with Gore, we can break the shadow's hold," he said.

"It's worth a try," said Ruby, eyes flashing with fire.

"Let's do it," said Danny.

The three of them turned and swept towards Gore like speeding arrows.

"If we attack from different angles, we'll have a better chance," Jack said.

Gore tipped his helmet back and watched them speed towards him without any sign of concern or panic.

Ruby rose above Gore's head, while Danny went low. Jack headed straight for his enemy. He heard a blast of sound and saw Gore's legs buckle under Danny's sonic attack. Then a stream of fire tore through the air, enveloping Gore's head. Jack gripped his sword firmly, and drove the blade deep into the shadow-figure's chest. Gore roared and spun, and for a moment Jack felt the cold shadow all around him. As the air cleared, he saw Gore was on his knees on the ground, head bowed.

"He's weakening!" Jack cried. "Again!"

But before any of them could regroup, a choking laughter filled the air. The General slowly stood up.

He straightened his back, drawing a deep breath. The shadows that formed his body ballooned outwards, and Jack's enemy began to grow.

And grow.

Jack looked on in horror as Gore

doubled, then tripled in size. As he did, the shadows became denser. His head rose above them; his arms grew thicker and more powerful. Soon he was ten storeys tall . . . no, twenty, dwarfing many of the buildings around him, his feet crushing cars like eggshells.

"*Weakening?*" chuckled General Gore. "I am just getting started!"

CHAPTER 6

LIGHT VS DARK

JACK STARED at his sunsteel blade, glinting in his hand. He had once slain General Gore with the powerful sword, but now it might as well have been a toothpick.

General Gore turned away from them and took a huge step, right into the middle of the river. It took him only one more step to reach the far bank. With a lazy swipe of his hand, he demolished a skyscraper. Then he lifted his arms, his voice like thunder. "Welcome your new ruler, humans!"

"What can we do?" asked Ruby, her face racked with horror.

"Make way for a *real* hero!"

It was Olly. He shot past, the Flameguard glowing in the dark.

"Olly, what are you doing here?" called Jack. "Wait! You'll get yourself killed!"

Jack flew after him, drawing up alongside as the wind whipped through their hair.

"I've got a secret weapon!" said Olly. Jack could see his eyes sparkling wildly. Under his skin, strange red veins coursed like fire.

"You weren't able to defeat him with the breastplate before," urged Jack.

"Not the breastplate," said Olly. "This!" He opened his hand to reveal the grey Starstone the elders had been constructing. "I *borrowed* it from Queen Felina."

Ruby and Danny joined them. "You mean you stole it!" said Ruby.

Danny made a grab for his arm, but Olly surged ahead. "Someone had to do *something*," he called back. "And

what better way to defeat Gore? The
Starstone is pure light. He's pure
shadow. One will cancel out the other."

General Gore was picking up the
remains of the bridge, laying it across
the river so his army could scramble
out of the water. He didn't see Olly

until he was a few metres away.

"You heroes really don't know when to give up, do you?" said the General.

"Ha!" yelled Olly, coming to a halt and hovering. "Try munching on this!"

He drew back his arm and hurled the grey stone at General Gore's head. It hit Gore's helmet with a dull thud, bounced off and fell to the ground far below.

"Oh," said Olly quietly. "I must have done it wrong."

General Gore reached out a hand but Olly just managed to slip beneath his grasping fingers. He flew down to where the Starstone had landed.

"I suppose I can rip the Flameguard from your corpse!" Gore said, and he lifted his foot, ready to stomp on Olly.

"No!" screamed Jack. He angled his body to fly down but knew he wouldn't make it in time. Even with the Flameguard, there was no way Olly could live through being trampled by the monster Gore had become. He saw Olly's terrified face as he looked up at the monstrous foot descending. Jack was still fifty metres away when a figure in a skysuit whipped across the ground, knocking Olly clear.

The foot slammed down, shaking the surrounding buildings.

The newcomer did not reappear.

Sickened, and confused, Jack stalled in the air and glanced up, wondering if one of his friends had somehow saved Olly. But Danny and Ruby were both above him.

General Gore lifted his foot, and Jack sucked in a breath. There on the ground lay the body of Queen Felina, dressed in a skysuit. *She saved Olly!*

She moved weakly, face contorted with pain, and horror filled Jack.

There's no way she can survive.

General Gore looked down at her and laughed. "How clumsy of me." He turned back to Olly, who was moving weakly on the ground. "Now, are you going to give me the Flameguard, or do you want to end up like her?"

Olly looked pale and terrified, frozen with the same shock that gripped Jack's body. But then something else on the ground seemed to draw his attention. Queen Felina's chest was glowing orange. Dimly at first, then brighter. She lifted an arm and the crackling surge of energy passed from her chest, along her fingers, then drifted into the air like a firefly. It seemed indecisive, moving in jerking streaks this way and that. Then it shot at lightning speed past Olly and collided with something on the ground.

The Starstone!

A flash of light, so bright Jack had to shield his eyes, exploded across the city. When he could see again past the dancing spots of colour, he saw the Starstone growing. It hovered above the ground, like something alive.

"No . . . " said Gore. "No, no, no . . . "

He staggered back as the orb of light swelled towards him, then he tripped, falling into a skyscraper and sending broken glass cascading to the ground.

A heart of fire, thought Jack. *It must mean courage. Queen Felina's bravery is the ingredient the Starstone was lacking!*

"Get it away from me!" Gore cried, trying to back away. But there was nowhere to go — the skyscraper shook but did not topple.

The surface of the glowing sphere continued towards him, and as it did, his shadow body cringed away like paper held to a fire. His limbs shrivelled and shrank, then turned to flickering flakes of ash. Gore's helmeted head was the last thing to be touched, crumpling in on itself and swallowing his wails of fear.

The new Starstone grew and rose higher, and as it did, rays of light seeped between the buildings and made the river sparkle. They washed over Gore's army, cleansing them of corruption, and swamped the shadows looming over the city, driving back the tendrils of darkness.

The Starstone rotated, then shot across the sky across the desert towards Solus. Jack used his visor to get a better view, and realised that the Starstone was speeding directly toward the Shadow Orb that rested on top of the Pyramid. Jack rose higher on his jetboots, holding his breath, wondering what would happen when the two met. The new Starstone collided with the old in a burst of spinning colours, and then the Shadow Orb was gone, replaced by the resplendent new sun.

And where, a moment ago, it had been night, day returned.

Jack's flare of joy was short-lived. With his friends at his side, he flew down slowly towards Queen Felina.

Gore was defeated, his shadows beaten back again. Khalea was safe.

But at what price?

● ● ●

Three days later, Jack stood on the plateau on top of the Great Pyramid of Solus, his head bowed, with Ruby and Danny at his side. Like the rest of the Team Hero contingent — those who weren't still recovering in the infirmary at Valour Station — they wore brand-new uniforms. The dignitaries of the four cities were dressed in their finest ceremonial robes to witness the coronation of their new ruler, Queen Panthera.

"I'll always think of her as Ms Steel," muttered Danny.

Chancellor Rex, who'd flown in for the ceremony, shot Danny a stern look, and he fell silent.

Professor Yokata, who leaned on

crutches near Danny, whispered, "I
will, too."

Jack took the opportunity to gaze
out over the four cities of Solus.
Reconstruction had halted for the
coronation, but he was amazed how
much they'd done already. Destroyed
buildings rose again in the skeletons
of scaffolding, and craftsmen had
begun resurrecting the four Guardian
statues that Gore had infected.

*This whole civilisation came within
a hair's breadth of collapse.*

As the jewelled crown was lowered
on to the new queen's head, Jack
noticed a silver tear escape down her

furred cheek. Many had perished to save Solus from Gore's domination, including Queen Felina and the elder of the Avaretti bird-people. The cities would rebuild, and injuries would mend, but there were deeper wounds that would take lifetimes to heal.

While the protective barrier that concealed Solus had been repaired, Jack wondered how much longer the secret cities could remain a secret. Many people in Khalea had witnessed the invasion of Gore's army. While Team Hero's contacts in the local government had come up with explanations for the attack and the bizarre creatures, Jack wasn't sure the people could forget what they had seen with their own eyes. Khalea too, would need to rebuild.

"People of Solus," said Queen Panthera, "my brave sister may no longer be with us in person, but her spirit will never leave. Each time you gaze up into the Starstone's light, think of her sacrifice, and remember her courage. I take this crown with a heavy heart, but I hope that I too can prove myself worthy of the honour. We must never be caught unprepared again. For too long we thought we were safe from evil, and protected from the outside world. Our arrogance was almost our undoing. If not for our allies in Team Hero, our cities would be no more."

Jack blushed, and saw that several of the dignitaries had turned towards the Team Hero attendees. Most were nodding respectfully.

"Now go back to your homes," said the new queen. "Celebrate with your families and rebuild your lives."

The crowd began to break apart, and Chancellor Rex came across to Jack and his friends. "You should be proud of yourselves," he said. "Ms Steel — I mean, Queen Panthera

— debriefed me on your role. I will
be recommending all of you for the
School Medal of Honour."

Jack felt his face flush even more.

"Does that mean we get first choice
in the canteen?" asked Danny.

The Chancellor flashed a brief smile, before regaining his composure. "Don't push your luck, Daniel."

"Any sign of Olly?" asked Ruby.

Chancellor Rex shook his head. "Nothing," he replied, "but our forces did pick up Bulk and Smarm. They're being held in the brig at Valour Station. So far, all they do is blame each other for getting caught."

"No surprises there," said Jack. He lowered his voice. "Do you really think Gore has gone for good this time?"

The Chancellor shrugged. "Perhaps, Jack, but if there's one thing history has taught us, it's that evil never sleeps for long. There will always be shadow waiting to arise again."

"And always a Chosen One to deal with it," said Ruby, nudging Jack.

He grinned at his friends. Through everything, they'd stuck by his side. The future was uncertain. Their enemies were defeated for now, but new dangers were never far away.

As long as Team Hero works together, we can take on any threat!

THE END

AD ON FOR A SNEA
EEK OF HOW IT ALL
BEGAN IN:

BATTLE FOR THE
HADOW SWORD

CHAPTER 1

BEAK THE FREAK

"HEY, BEAK, are you cold or something?" shouted Ricky Evans.

Jack Beacon pretended not to hear. He walked at the back of the group, staring up at the soaring steel skyscrapers of Ventura City. Their windows reflected the bright sun like blazing mirrors.

"Yeah, take your gloves off, freak," called Ricky's friend Olivia.

Jack had heard it all before. He fought the urge to shout something back, remembering what his dad always said — *Just ignore them, Jack.* By the time they got to the City Museum, they'd be bored and the taunts would stop.

His teacher, Mr Parry, stopped to let Jack catch up with him. "Keep up, Jack," he said, rolling his eyes.

"Yes, sir," said Jack.

Besides, he *was* a freak. "Beak the Freak," as the bullies liked to chant. Even the doctors he'd seen couldn't explain what was wrong with his hands.

When they reached the road, the lights changed and Jack and Mr Parry had to wait. The rest of the class were already crossing the square towards the grand columns in front of the City Museum. As Jack watched them, he felt an odd prickle across his neck. Then he noticed someone on the bench opposite....

CHECK OUT BOOK ONE:
BATTLE FOR
THE SHADOW SWORD
to find out what happens next!

IN EVERY BOOK OF
TEAM HERO SERIES
ONE there is a special
Power Token. Collect
all four tokens to get
an exclusive Team Hero
Club pack. The pack
contains everything you and
your friends need to form your
very own Team Hero Club.

FREE TEAM HERO CLUB PACK

MEMBERSHIP CARDS · MEMBERSHIP CERTIFICATE · STICKERS · POWER GAME · BOOKMARKS

Just fill in the form below, send it in with your four tokens
and we'll send you your Team Hero Club Pack.

SEND TO: Team Hero Club Pack Offer, Hachette Children's Books,
Marketing Department, Carmelite House, 50 Victoria Embankment,
London, EC4Y 0DZ.

CLOSING DATE: 31st December 2018

WWW.TEAMHEROBOOKS.CO.UK

- - - - - - - - - - - - - - - ✂ - - - - - - - - - - - - - - -

Please complete using capital letters *(UK and Republic of Ireland residents only)*

FIRST NAME
SURNAME
DATE OF BIRTH
ADDRESS LINE 1
ADDRESS LINE 2
ADDRESS LINE 3
POSTCODE
PARENT OR GUARDIAN'S EMAIL

I'd like to receive Team Hero email newsletters and information about
other great Hachette Children's Group offers (I can unsubscribe at any time)

*Terms and conditions apply. For full terms and conditions please go to
teamherobooks.co.uk/terms*

*TEAM HERO Club packs
available while stocks last.
Terms and conditions apply.*

COLLECT ALL OF SERIES TWO!